The Demon
in the Dark

A play

by Peter Lancett

illustrated by Jan Pedroietta

Ransom

The Demon in the Dark
The Players

 Narrator
(80 words)

 The Dark Man
(47 words)

 Girl
(33 words)

 Angel
(30 words)

 The Old Man
(12 words)

The Demon in the Dark
The Acts

1

Act One:
Wake Up!

Narrator:
The Old Man talks to the Dark Man.

The Old Man:
A girl will come to you.
You must do as she says.

Narrator:
The Dark Man waits for the girl.

Girl:
Wake up!

The Dark Man:
I am awake.

Narrator:

The girl hands a note to the Dark Man.

Girl:

Read this. There is a demon in the city.

2 Act Two:
The Girl's Power

Narrator:
The Dark Man has read the note.

The Dark Man:
I need to hold your hand.

17

Girl:

Yes, I must share my power
with you.

The Dark Man:
My hands are melting!

Girl:
Your hands are OK.

The Dark Man:
Wow, that was strange.

Girl:
The power I gave you will protect you. Now go.

3
Act Three:
Angel

Narrator:
The Dark Man waits in a coffee shop.

Narrator:
A girl stands by the Dark Man's table.

The Dark Man:
Did the Old Man send you?

Angel:

My name is Angel. I can lead you to the demon.

Narrator:
Angel has taken them to a tunnel under the ground.

Angel:
The demon is down there.

The Dark Man:
Are you coming with me? You are a real angel, I can tell.

Angel:
I cannot go. I am afraid.

The Dark Man:
Do not worry. I have the
power to kill the demon.

Narrator:

The Dark Man goes to kill the demon. Angel speaks inside his mind.

Angel:

Never worry. I shall watch over you. Always.

Narrator:
 The Dark Man knows he
 will beat the demon
 now ...

More **Dark Man** books:

Stories

Plays